Scrivener Jones is a journalist for the Seattle Picayune, living in and reporting from the town of Kahnaway, deep in the middle of the Olympic Peninsula.

As a child, Scrivener's parents made her join the Kahnaway Beaver Patrol, which they thought was a fun nature group for kids, similar to the Girl Scouts, but which was actually an ultra-feminist survivalist militia, who were gracious and kind, but incredibly confused about how and why this nine-year-old girl started suddenly showing up for knife training and meetings about forcibly castrating the patriarcy.

Kahnaway — pt13
A Trip Into Murder

by P. Calavara

People always think it's "Naughty Ned", but it's not. Ned wasn't "Naughty," he was "Nouty," quite aside from your feelings about superfluous silent letters and the fact that he always tried to bang me[1]. So. Nouty Ned. A close enough distinction that people inevitably heard wrong when they first met him, to which he inevitably replied, "Please, call me Nouty Ned. Naughty Ned was my father," before laughing uproariously. Every. Time.

You know that kid in high school who *loved* prog rock and metal, and somehow always seemed to have acid? The guy who only watched British television on PBS, had the weird import version of his favorite albums, and who always chose *Toadlicker69* as his screenname? Well, that was Ned. I'd actually known him before high school, when he was still named Jim, and was a straight-A student, pretty smart, easily bored, and already living in a total dreamworld about his charm — before his rechristening at the altar

---

[1] I didn't take it personally. He tries to bang everyone.

of mind expansion between 8th and 9th grade. That summer break Jim dropped acid for the first time, and when the first day of high school rolled around, Nouty Ned showed up. Of course, it took quite a while for people to adjust to calling him by his new moniker, probably some still don't, though I had the graciousness to start immediately. He'd been one of the few people in middle school to never make fun of me about *my* name, so what the hell, right?

In high school he had self-styled himself as a sort of hero-figure to the various counter-culture kids: the skaters and the slackers, the hip-hop heads and the drama nerds, the punks and the early-onset hipsters. Of course, Ned was nobody's hero except in his own mind, but don't take that to mean that he was purely an object of ridicule. Nouty Ned was friend to pretty much every teen who didn't go to high school football games, *not even during Homecoming.* Ned was easygoing, completely non-judgmental, full of weird facts, and was a fair bass player when he wasn't high. Still, though, he was probably most well-known and popular for his skill in acquisitions. Nouty Ned was the dude who could get you *anything.* He was the school's ready supply of contraband: pot, psychedelics, switchblades, Japanese porn, and the more extreme firecrackers like M-80s and cherry bombs. Nouty Ned sold me my first butterfly knife.

Once high school ended, so, basically, did our friendship. We would occasionally see each other for a friendly greeting and a quick chat at parties and around town during the college years, before the link was severed completely when I left town forever. It wasn't until right after I was forced to move back to Kahnaway that I ran into him again while I was buying bear spray at the surplus store.

"Scrivener Jones?!? Holy hell!" his scratchy whine, unchanged twenty years on, hit me like an algebra book. "I can't believe it! I had heard you were eaten by a gila monster!"

"Nouty Ned," I replied, turning to my erstwhile compatriot. I turned to discover that, for better or worse, he had not changed a whit since high school — same wispy black goatee, same platinum hair, same pale skin on a gaunt frame, probably even the same Metallica shirt worn in the same ironic style. "I can't believe you're not dead. Or in prison."

"You and my grandma both!" We hugged in the way of old friends. "What brings you back to town? Visiting your folks?"

"Work. I was transferred here for my job."

"Oh? What do you do? You have to tell me if you're a cop," he smiled devilishly, kidding, but not kidding.

"That's not true. It's a lie the police planted on television to trick people into self-incriminating," I said. "But I'm not a cop. I'm in the journalism racket. I'm a reporter for *The Seattle Picayune*."

"A journalist? Hot damn! That's perfect! What are you doing this Saturday?"

And thus began my strange working relationship with Nouty Ned — The Kahnaway Psychonaut.

A psychonaut, if you've never heard the term[2], is a person who explores altered states of consciousness. According to Ned, this is sometimes accomplished through things like meditation or lucid dreaming, but it's most often accomplished through experimenting with mind-altering drugs. This isn't teens experimenting at house parties, mind, this is chemists and explorers experimenting with creating and searching for new molecules and compounds to see if they'll get you high. Ned was one such explorer.

Now, some of these explorers are corporate chemists, working in high-end laboratories, developing new synthetics — a difficult endeavour requiring patience, exactitude, and resources, none of which were qualities that Ned had in abundance.

Some of these explorers were bathtub chemists, working in makeshift labs, experimenting with chemicals — a difficult endeavour requiring knowledge, meticulousness, and ingenuity, none of which were qualities that Ned had in abundance.

So if Ned wasn't a chemist, what was he? Well, Ned was the third kind of exploratory chemist.

See, what Ned lacked in scientific rigor he made up for with an unwavering willingness to lick *anything*.

Just as some dude had essentially just started licking toads until one of them made him trip the light fantastic, Nouty Ned was the guy who was willing to take the first plunge. There were a number of labs in the region, both clandestine and not, that he guinea-pigged for, taking that first mysterious dose to see what would happen, but he also did his own experiments

 [2] I hadn't.

with natural materials, ingesting strange molds, smoking salamander-piss tinctures, or drinking magic-mushroom-infused kombucha. Ned was absolutely convinced that the entire world was full of psychedelics just waiting to be discovered: Mysterious mushrooms to smoke! Tantalizing amphibians to kiss! Enigmatic bugs to eat! Surely *some* of these were a gateway to the promised land, and Ned was game for all of it.

All in all, just good wholesome fun, right?

Nouty Ned wasn't alone in his explorations — he was a member of a thriving internet community of the like-minded; self-styled explorers of the unknown, posting and sharing their explorations for the betterment of mankind. The community ran the gamut from armchair toadlickers like Ned to chemists working at the very highest level of their field — talking Nobel Prize level.

I followed the group's goings-on at the most casual level that could be accomplished while still counting as paying attention — logging in and lurking when I was bored or needed something to put me to sleep, or, as now, checking in when Ned had contacted me about observing him on an exploration.

So, you're probably wondering what the hell I've got to do with any of this. Good question! My readers are so smart and handsome! Well, one of the psychonaut community's guidelines is that its members should have an *unbiased and sober observer* whenever they attempt to travel beyond the paper-thin walls of this reality and into the great beyond. This was, first and foremost, for the obvious safety reasons: adverse reactions, accidental poisonings, exposure, wandering into danger, trying to make out with wolves, etc. But having an observer was also to help provide an unbiased and impartial verification of the experiments — at least to the extent that an outside observer can verify a guy claiming that he can now speak the language of the daffodils or feel how money smells in an enlightening new way.

My occasional role, then, was as Nouty Ned's observer. He would call me up semi-regularly to see if I was willing to take a hike into the woods with him while he ingested some crazy shit or other, and a few times a year I would agree to join him, times when I needed a break from the world or felt like watching a grown man chew on what he assured me was bigfoot scat that he had found at a clandestine marijuana grow and then parboiled.

This particular expedition was on a January Saturday, late in the morning after an early lunch. Kahnaway had been hit by fresh snow the night before, with the depth ebbing and flowing from the city center, where it was just an inch or two, to several inches the further away you travelled in the valley. I drove, since I was the one who wasn't hoping to go tripping balls on distilled slug residue or lab-grade elutriated microwave mold. Ned navigated and fiddled with the treble and bass knobs on my stereo[3]. We headed west through the lowlands and hills of the valley, dotted with wilderness and farms, mostly orchards, but with a surprising number of llama ranches and a steady stream of tourist traps.

 [3] Obviously he was one of *those* guys.

Eventually, we hit the area where the forest meets the field — a sort of disputed zone between civilization and one of the darkest wilds in North America. Locals called it *The DMZ*. Part of this was due to the ongoing skirmishes between the townies and the rangers of the national park service, who never quite got over discovering a flourishing urban area smack dab in the middle of one of their shiniest jewels, and while this led to occasional legal disputes and gun battles, this demilitarized zone was primarily about a larger conflict — the war between folk and forest.

People cannot help but keep trying to build, ever on, ever up. We're an all-consuming amoeba, gobbling and growing uncontrollably. We push the borders of what nature has allowed us to have, pouring our concrete and putting our homes closer and closer to the green. This is true everywhere, but in Kahnaway the forest is one of the wilds that has chosen to fight back. We build our trails and roads, our farms and homes, pushing out and chopping down, attempting to hold ground against nature, or to at least form enough of a *détente* to survive. Many of them don't make it. The trees return, and the winds howl as the wolves circle, and the structure is reduced to wreck and abandonment[4]. But not all of them suffer this fate. Some of the homes and buildings survive the encroachment of the woods, the dark winters, and the occasional arson attempts by angry drunken forest rangers. I have never understood why some homes stand while others are consumed. Maybe there's an algorithm. Maybe it's all about location. Maybe it's

---

[4] Becoming, of course, an abandoned insane asylum.

all about knowing which forest spirits to worship and which to fear. Maybe it's just luck.

We left the paved road for a gravel one, pushing past thicker woods that blocked out the skies, before coming to a large open area packed with short trees and a bright white sky. I pulled over at a wide spot in the road at Ned's instruction, and we donned our gloves and warm hats before leaving the relative warmth of the car. Our backpacks and folding chairs came out from the backseat, and we continued a short ways up the road on foot, before taking a likely-looking trail. The woods here felt like a Christmas tree farm gone to seed, which it quite possibly may have been. We were surrounded by 10-12ft tall trees, mostly pine, growing close together and filling up every direction we looked but up — their thick branches billowing out at person level, making it impossible to see very far, but without any of the sky or light being blocked.

I should emphasize that no matter how this may read, absolutely *nothing* about this trip was conducted in silence. Nouty Ned moved through life with a constant clip of chatter pouring from his mouth. Ned was, of course, the kind of guy who knew something about everything, found all of it fascinating, and felt the compulsive need to discuss it all *right now*. This isn't to imply that some of it wasn't interesting and he did actually listen to other people's opinions provided they could get a word in edgewise, which is more than you can say for a lot of people. Plus, he could be a great fount of information when I needed it, and not just on how to emulsify banana peel sap to create a potent smokable. Ned read compulsively, retained it like a motherfucker, and had connections all throughout the Cascadian underworld — not, like, the dark world of organized crime and contract killings, but the far more interesting land of pirate radio, black markets, and illicit science. Unfortunately, trying to pry specific information out of him always ran the grave risk of losing an hour to having the polyrhythms of Captain Beefheart albums mansplained to you, or having to listen to an exhaustive blow-by-blow of his latest D&D campaign before he finally answered whatever question you'd asked him. Or, for example, one time, when I desperately needed the contact information for an amateur bombmaker named *The Petard,* he had made me take dictation on his high-flying thesis on why the British version of things were algorithmically superior to the American remakes.

We continued walking on the trail until we were a solid quarter mile from the road, where our little deer trail opened up to a small clearing, maybe fifteen feet in diameter, almost entirely devoid of plants. Ned claimed that this was the spot for his explorations — he'd been here before, and really liked the aura, the feng shui, and something or other about ley lines or crop circles or some other junk. We set out our folding chairs, mine a red canvas camping chair, his a sort of collapsible beach recliner thing. Ned planted some candles and incense into the snow around his chair, *just so.* Probably some crystals, too.

The clearing would have been charming any time of year, but draped in snow, it had a hauntingly ethereal beauty. White tree branches, not quite overburdened to the point of drooping, held themselves up, with green tips penetrating the white in bursts of splendor, the trunks barely visible as splashes of dark paint on a white canvas. The ground was covered in the sort of shimmering snow that left an unbroken illusion of endlessness up until the area directly beneath each tree, which looked like little caves, each one housing its own secret world. If only Ned would quit talking about hypothetical Ultraman adaptations, it would have been easy to get lost in this little enclave, to believe it was the only place in existence.

I set up Ned's video recorder on its tripod as Ned settled into his seat and readied his concoction — probably something to do with a particular kind of mold that grew on the roots of salmonberries or possibly a tincture made from those weird new pinky-blue jellyfish that had been improbably swimming upstream from the Sound to beach themselves on our local riverbeds.

Once he was ready, I hit record and Nouty Ned introduced himself, then began his lengthy explanation of the exploration he was about to embark upon. I settled into my own chair, paying little or no attention to his soliloquy, though I wish I'd listened better, because I swear to god I overheard him saying something about making tea from the pellet of an owl who had been eating mice that had been raised on a steady diet of peyote.

Formalities out of the way, Ned poured a cup of steaming thick liquid from a stainless steel thermos, held it up to the camera, then tipped it back, savoring every last drop while grimacing at the taste and trying not to throw up. Once it was finished, he leaned back in his beach chair, pulled his headphones over his ears, and closed his eyes, attempting to let the potential hallucinogen wash over him.

I settled into my own chair, and, finally in silence, enjoyed the serenity of the space, listening to the occasional chitter of a bird or the settling of the snow as I closed my eyes to let winter take over my soul, entering into a deep meditation. After a minute or two of that, I pulled out my notebook, one of those old-style college-rule things with the black and white mottled covers, and set to writing, pausing every few minutes to check that Ned was still breathing.

> *It was winter in Kahnaway, which meant that all road construction had come to a screeching halt for the season. The Tinpot Dictator — the middle-aged big-haired charging-boar of a woman who had been ruling the roundabout construction site near my house with an iron fist — had suddenly found her authority stripped away from her for the time being. The loss of power was beginning to get to her, and the situation was becoming untenable.*
>
> *At home, of course, she controlled every aspect of her family's life, running it much as she ran the construction site. She directed every movement her children and husband took: dictating when they had finished one activity*

and could move to another, prescribing exactly what they ate for every meal, determining which sock went on which foot, and even regulating the times and durations of their toilet use. This wasn't enough, though. Controlling family was fine, but couldn't come anywhere near filling the hole in her heart left from having ultimate control over hundreds or thousands of strangers on a daily basis.

But where could she possibly get that kick during the winter months? Volunteering at the library had seemed like a possibility, so she had given it a go, bringing a special whistle to screech on whenever anyone had dared make a sound. Whispering? WHISTLE! Stepping too loudly? WHISTLE! Typing on the computer terminal? WHISTLE! It got her close, but there was a problem. It turns out that to get any real *power* in the library you needed a lot of education, leaving her outranked left and right by librarians with advanced degrees and PhDs in library science. Her move for dominance over the regional branch through her terror campaign of aggressive whistling had been countered by the regular librarians, with their fancy doctorates, forcing her to call them doctor. Checked back into her place as a volunteer, the Tinpot Dictator fumed, but was clever enough to know that she had been beaten this round. This would never do, and so, after a final shift spent rearranging the card catalogue, hiding all the dictionaries, *and taking a literal dump in the book return, she looked at other options.*

Taking a position as a prison guard seemed like the solution for a while — treating the incarcerated like her personal playthings, controlling every aspect of their lives, pitting them against each other in pitched battles in the yard just for kicks. She had loved it! It was nearly perfect! But there was a problem — unless she lived at the prison, on duty 24/7, then inevitably the next shift, guards with their own agendas, would undo her plans and schemes as part of implementing their own whenever she was off-duty. And don't even get me started on the warden! That guy had no patience for schemes other than his own.

The Tinpot Dictator watched the snow from her kitchen window, sulking as she watched her five year old carefully count Cheerios, making sure he didn't take more or less than she had instructed him to. She was definitely in a funk. What else was there that would allow her to hold the unchecked power of life and death in her hands? Had the time finally come for her to enter a career in—

Something made a noise — through the trees not too far from us — and I looked up from my writing. I sat silently, waiting for it to happen again. It sounded like someone talking. Had it been someone talking? I looked over at Nouty Ned, who was snoring peacefully. Wait! There it was again! Definitely talking, but I couldn't make out the words, I couldn't even make out enough to tell if it was English.

I quietly put my writing away, back in my bag to keep it dry and safe, in spite of its pure uncut ridiculousness. I tried to be as silent as possible, waiting to pick up any more noises that might be made. I suppose I could have just called out, but that seemed ill-advised, since I had no idea who was out there. I wasn't totally sure whose land we were on, which could always make things awkward. Was it someone's private property? Someone who was about to find us and then have to make a decision on either giving us some cocoa or hunting us for sport? Or had we accidentally strayed into the national park, about to encounter a group of park rangers on the prowl — looking for townies to murder as part of the brutal initiation rituals new rangers had to go through to earn their merit badges?

I stepped softly to Ned, and put my hand to his softly slumbering forehead, I guess checking to make sure he wasn't feverish? I dunno. I suppose I could have checked his breathing or taken his pulse or something, too, but if he wanted that kind of service, he should have been friends with a nurse. I decided he was fine.

The snow was soft enough to mask even my fumbling footsteps in silence as I made my way in the direction the voices had come from. I felt like a ghost in a ghostly place, passing silently between the snowy trees as a spirit. It was less comforting to know that anyone stalking us would have been equally silent, and in spite of my heavy coat, I shivered. If you had asked me what I had hoped to accomplish by investigating a strange noise, I'm not sure that I could have answered exactly. Was it caution? Curiosity? Boredom?

Not far from the space where Ned and I had set up, I pushed past some especially dense trees, to find myself suddenly in a large clearing, having passed abruptly beyond the treeline. This was a real clearing, nothing like the thin open patch where Ned was still sleeping. I was in a snow-covered, featureless, rectangle, surrounded by a wall of pine trees, with a strange centerpiece: a copse of birch trees planted in a ring about twenty feet in diameter in the center — like a fairy circle, but with trees instead of mushrooms. And there, in that birch tree circle, was a dead body.

It took me a moment to realize that the unmoving object in the snow was a person, crumpled in the snow, and not just, I guess, a pile of garbage dressed in a peacoat. My blood was already running cold, but, perhaps shamefully, a jolt of excitement — probably fear and adrenaline, right? — warmed me some. I stood there on the edge of the trees, dead still but for my eyes, which scanned hurriedly for signs of anyone or anything else in the clearing. I exhaled slowly as I concluded that I was on my own, then slowly, silently, retreated backwards until I was again hidden behind the trees. I circled the clearing slowly, moving through the trees, cautiously, until I came to a place in the treeline that allowed me slightly better cover from which to hide and examine the scene.

The ring of birch trees were all mature, fully grown and forming a natural grotto, and must, I could only assume, have been planted that way on purpose in the semi-distant past. On several sides of the grotto were what looked like snow covered benches, and in the center was something large that I couldn't make out under the snow — a fountain, maybe? We'll go with that. What was this strange place?

From my new, closer, vantage point, I could tell that the corpse was definitely a corpse, or at least a critically injured person, spread on the ground, face down beside the fountain, with a knife in its back. It looked like a large man from where I was hiding, dressed in a thick dark navy blue long coat, which hid any blood. His pants struck me as odd for a reason I couldn't place, at least not from hiding in the bushes thirty feet away. He was shoeless, with thick woolen socks — there was a single leather boot, beside his feet. I couldn't see his face, but the skin I could see was a pale peach, and his hair was jet black, not dark brown, beneath a grey watch cap. The knife in his back was actually a dagger, and an odd-looking one at that — was that a serpentine blade? — like something stupid and ceremonial from a genre film. One of his arms was slung up on the side of the fountain, while the other was reaching towards something dark in the snow that I couldn't make out from where I was. The missing boot, maybe? No, too small.

I pursed my lips, unsure of what to do[5]. I knew that I needed to see if he was still alive, but I had no

---

[5] I had obviously left my cursed phone back in the car, not that it mattered, there was no signal out here and my phone was only making outgoing calls to the Idaho RNC this week.

idea if it was safe to move out into the open. I listened for the sounds of anyone else in the area, but there was only deathly silence. I shivered, as I again thought of the same soft snow that disguised my own passage doing the same for anyone else sneaking up on me. On top of that, if I walked over to the clearing would I be leaving a trail to myself in the snow? Even if the murderer wasn't currently present — a big *if* — if they returned would they see and then *follow* my footprints back to me? Maybe if I ventured out I could brush away my footprints, Danny-in-the-hedgemaze style? As I tried to reason this out, I realized that I didn't see any other footprints in the clearing. Why not? Had the body been here since before the last snow? Unlikely — there was no snow on the corpse. So were the corpse's footsteps, the murderer's footsteps, just not visible from where I was? Had they been brushed away? Where should footsteps even be, if there were any?

The birch trees, thirteen of them, were set close together, though not too close, since they were trees. There was a larger opening on one side, behind the corpse's feet. Was there a pathway? There must be, right? This was clearly a *place*. Someone or someones had made this place for some reason, so it stood to reason that there must have been a way to get here besides the blundering passage through the woods that I had taken. Was there a house in the area? I let my eyes wander, going slack as they drifted across the clearing — there it was. A break in the treeline off to my right, with two large snow-covered objects on either side of the gap. They had just registered as snow-covered bushes and a thin spot before, but now I could see it. So this was the path that led to this place. Had the victim walked in that way, then been stabbed in the back? There was no cover, so he must have known someone was there with him, right?

I decided to quickly experiment with footsteps. Still behind the trees, I took some steps, then attempted to brush them back to just snow with a fallen branch. It did a so-so job… fine if the snow was already broken up enough, less good on something pure. The snow between me and the birch trees was something in between. I briefly considered trying to walk over *en pointe*, placing only immaculate dainty steps in the snow, leaving only the perfect imitations of deerprints, but discarded this scheme as impractical for about a dozen reasons that I'm sure you can pretty easily guess. What do rampaging buffalo prints look like? Maybe I could imitate those.

Sighing, I circled back around the trees, until I could see further down the snow-covered path into the clearing, but it wound around too much to see where it came from, and there was nothing of immediate interest there. I briefly entertained taking it, but dismissed the thought almost immediately — this is where the murderer most likely came from and went, right? I went back to my spot closer to the corpse, and, from there, carefully moved out into the open, trying to take as few steps as possible, stepping into places where the snow had already been somewhat disturbed by natural causes. Moving this way, I made the birch tree circle by one of the benches, and crouched there on my haunches, studying the body from closer up.

I could see more of the corpse's face from here — its aquiline nose and rough brow, cast dark with the pallor of death. The eyes were open, flat blue orbs that might as well have had Xs drawn over them. At the very least, I thought, I can abandon the chase without worrying about leaving a wounded man to die.

Now that I could really see it, the dagger looked even more ridiculous than before: a gilded handle complete with embedded gems, a hilt that curved impractically, atop a twisted blade that looked like it was probably made of silver with weird arcane symbols carved into it. It seemed like such a frivolous thing, a prime example of just-too-muchery, but there was no doubt that it was stabbed into this guy, so I guess that proves something about the danger of *all* knives, no matter how ostentatious or silly they appear to the naked eye. There was no blood on the part of the knife I could see, or in the snow around it, or anywhere, actually. It was all safely pooling within the body's winter clothes, I guess? Was that normal? I wasn't sure, since I'm not an expert in blood spatter analysis[6].

The dark item on the ground beside the outstretched arm was a gun, but not one that made any sense. It looked like one of those old flintlock black powder style things that you might use in a duel if you'd spent the night combining way too much cocaine and *Hamilton*. It must be a toy, right? Next to the body was a sealed yellow envelope. Something sticking out from under the body appeared to be pink and lacy — maybe

---

[6] I *am* however, a certified coffee stain analyst.

a woman's handkerchief? Was the corpse clutching a pocket watch that had stopped somehow at the precise moment of his death? I couldn't tell, but the whole thing felt so surreal and orchestrated, that it wouldn't have surprised me. What the hell was going on?

Checking for any footprints the killer might have left, I saw that the snow around the corpse had been suitably defiled by action, but then muddled up to hide anything like a proper identifying bootprint. Immediately beyond the corpse I could see where tracks had been brushed to oblivion, forming a rough trail heading back out of the grove and down the path beyond the treeline. From here I could see that the snow-covered objects beside the break in the trees were actually stone gargoyles[7]. Would my snow trail be so obvious? Was I only noticing the mussed trail of footprints because I was looking for it?

Okay, I was ready to be done playing Nancy Drew. This guy looked pretty damned dead, so it was time for me to bail, pack up Nouty Ned, and go find some cops or at least some cocoa.

I made my way back from the birch copse, carefully obliterating my footsteps in the snow, and had made it about three-fourths of the way when I stopped — voices. I could hear them close by, just beyond the trees, and getting louder. I abandoned the precision of my work, and hoped that nobody would notice or bother looking for footprints this far from the scene, then quickly hid back behind the dense treeline, peeking out through the branches as a group of people appeared.

 [7] As opposed to the more popular cotton candy gargoyles? -ed

Seven people in all entered the clearing, passing between the stone gargoyles, having some meaningless discussion about, like, pinochle or polo or some other such bullshit. There were four men and three women, and they were dressed heavily for the winter of a bygone era. Three of the men wore long, dark coats and tall hats, while the women wore heavy fur-lined jackets that brought the word *ermine* to my thoughts, unbidden. One of the women wore a wide-brimmed hat, adorned heavily with cloth flowers, another wore a sort of baby blue cloche, and the third, I shit you not, wore a pink bonnet. The final member of the group was bare-headed, and dressed in tails.

"*Great Scott!*" roared the man in front, as he entered the birch tree grotto.

"Good lord, it's Sir Edward!" exclaimed a second man, gesticulating wildly at the corpse.

One of the women, the one with the flowered hat, let out something halfway between a shriek and a scream, while the one in the bonnet appeared to faint away, falling into the arms of the man closest to her. The third woman put her hand to her mouth, a quizzical look on her face.

The man in front was a large fellow with a long Van Dyke beard showing the barest hints of grey, which curved out from his chin, below wire spectacles and a black top hat. His long coat was pinstriped with a fur collar, and even from my distant vantage and through some trees, I could tell that it cost more than my car, though at least half of that is about my car.

The second man was similarly dressed in a

fancy fur-lined coat, but with different facial hair, the sideburn to mustache look — something the internet informed me is called an *A La Souvarov*.

The third man, the one who caught the fainting woman, was clean-shaven, with a hat that wasn't quite so tall as the others', and was wearing something more like a long shearling jacket.

The two bearded men moved closer to the body, and the woman in the cloche hat held up a hand, saying "Careful, now. We do not want to obliterate any footprints or other evidence of this heinous crime."

Souvarov paused, but *Van Dyke* continued as if he hadn't heard, stepping to the corpse, then falling back onto his haunches beside it. He reached out a paw, and gently shook the body. "Dead as a doornail."

"Poor soul," exclaimed the *Floral Hat*, as she held a hanky to her eyes. "I wonder what he called us all out here to tell us."

"Calling us all out into this dreadful weather just to find he's killed himself! I must say, bad show! I had thought the man better than that, what with his blood being what it is," remarked *Souvarov*, as he rubbed his arms for warmth.

"'Killed himself'? *Really*, Uncle!" the *Cloche* replied, giving the man a shove, somewhere between friendly and chastening. "This was clearly murder most foul."

Souvarov harrumphed. "It can hardly be said that a man who hasn't sense enough to not be murdered on such a day didn't bring this upon himself."

"Spoken like a man with a guilty conscience, my

friend," *Van Dyke* replied, looking up at his compatriot.

"Are we sure he's dead?" asked *Floral Hat*, suddenly, optimistically. "Perhaps it is just a wound?"

Van Dyke shook his head. "A mortal wound, I am afraid. The queen will be most distraught at this death. The man had a certain queerness to him, for truth, yet remained a favored cousin of hers. I do not look forward to breaking the news."

"Well," said *Cloche*, thoughtfully, "perhaps we can assuage her hurt some with the balm of discovering who has done this disgraceful thing to poor dead Sir Edward."

"Capital idea, daughter!" agreed *Van Dyke*. "Surely such men — and women — of breeding such as we have everything we need here with us to determine the course of events and the guilty party. Preston!" the man called.

"Sir?" the man without a hat replied, stepping forward.

"Send the boy to fetch the constabulary, and then bring us some proper thinking drinks for the weather — something brash — and toddies for the ladies, of course."

"Immediately, sir," the butler said with a curt bow, and then vanished back behind the trees.

"Good man," *Van Dyke* nodded.

Cloche watched the butler leave, even stepping back through the trees to look after him, before turning back to the assembled people. "How well do you know your new man, father?"

"New? Why — he has been with me four

months now, and I have no reason to question him," *Van Dyke* replied, somewhat taken aback.

"Hmm… And what again happened to your previous valet?"

Van Dyke began to answer, but a stirring moan stopped him.

"Oh! Virginia is coming back around!" said the clean-shaven man who had been holding the fainted woman in the bonnet this entire time. "There, there, poor thing. You've had a shock."

Virginia put a hand to her forehead, while remaining ensconced in the man's arms, "I had the most dreadful vision…"

"'Tis no vision, I'm afraid, dearie," *Van Dyke* said resolutely. "Sir Edward is dead, murdered here on our family lands, and one among us perhaps the culprit, for who else could have made it onto the grounds?" He gestured grandly towards the hills and woods and, I hoped only coincidentally, to my hiding place. I shivered — that eerie feeling of someone walking over your grave.

"Come now, brother, must you be so ghoulish?" *Floral Hat* opined, still pale and upset over finding a dead body for some reason. "Surely it was not one of this party, but some random assassin."

"An assassin! *Here?* Oh! I feel I may faint again!" Virginia swooned, but remained standing.

The clean-shaven man took her hand. "There there, Virginia. You are safe."

"An assassin sounds interesting," remarked *Cloche*, cooly.

Souvarov nodded. "No doubt here to further their anarchist political agenda, or a rival of Sir Edward's in some other affair, business perhaps, or his well-known interest in the occult, sent here to wrest information from the man."

Van Dyke stroked his beard thoughtfully. "Except that who but we six knew Sir Edward was here?"

"Your Preston knew," murmured *Cloche*, though *Van Dyke* pointedly ignored the remark.

"Oh? Where was dear Sir Edward to have been?" asked *Floral Hat*.

"Why — wintering in Budapest with the *Infanta*, of course! I exchanged letters with him a mere ten days past, when he left every indication of staying on there through the spring. Imagine, then, to travel here in secret, and incognito no less! I myself did not recognize him at the door! Really! It's just too much!"

"Well, if not an assassin, then a drifter! Dear Sir Edward must have caught him sneaking upon the grounds to strump from the orchard or to poach your game!" *Floral Hat* surmised with dark enthusiasm.

"No, dear sister, I find it unlikely." *Van Dyke* shook his head, "How could a drifter have made it over the fences without alerting our dogs? This man was murdered..." pause for effect, "...by one of us!"

Virginia let out another little shriek, and there would have been a stroke of thunder if the weather had been right. I shook my head in confusion. Dogs? Fences? I had obviously encountered neither. What the hell was he talking about?

"You beast!" *Floral Hat* smacked *Van Dyke* on the shoulder. "What a horrible thing to say! As if one of us could indeed be a murderer!"

"Or the butler," *Cloche* muttered again with a smile, as she moved towards the body, kneeling beside it, presumably to search for clues. "Father, is this not one of the dueling pistols you keep locked in the desk in your study?"

"Indeed it is, but please, daughter, I implore you, do not go near the body. It is most unladylike and I fear for your soul and your welfare should you encounter such evil as this."

Cloche ignored the entreaty, and continued to examine the corpse. "Oh, father, do stop being so silly and provincial. How else are we to infer motive or suspects without examining the clues?"

Van Dyke harrumphed, "Your mother, God rest her soul, was right about why you have not yet found a husband, dear Bernadette."

Holy shit! I peered through the trees and snow with narrow eyes and wide suspicion— was that guy actually *my mother in a fake beard???*

Bernadette, the woman in the cloche hat, rolled her eyes — I assume, since I couldn't see her face — and continued looking at the corpse. "What knife is this? I feel as though I have encountered its like before."

"Why, that blade is a ceremonial one from the Fraternal Ord—" *Clean-shaven* began to say before a series of grunts and throat clearings and furious hand gestures from *Van Dyke* and *Souvarov* cut him off. "Aww, yes, pardon me. I meant to say that that is a very strange knife, which was definitely *not* used by any secret societies and probably was in fact discovered by Sir Edward on his many travels in Eastern Europe, or perhaps to the Indian subcontinent."

"How dreadfully savage!" Virginia shivered, just as Preston appeared at the trail head with a tray of beverages. Bernadette eyed him warily, and I found myself studying him as well. Something about the man was tickling some memory that I couldn't quite place.

"Perhaps this will warm madame," the butler spoke like a man from central casting, as he handed the woman a steaming glass of hot toddy, complete with lemon slice and cinnamon stick. He doled out the drinks, serving the women before handing the men what I assumed were brandies. He turned to *Van Dyke*, standing resolutely at attention, as he said "The constable has been summoned, sir."

"Very good, very good," *Van Dyke* nodded, before dismissing the man with a wave of the hand. Bernadette watched him go with narrow eyes. I wracked my mind, but couldn't place him.

"Praytell, where is Sir Edward's boot?" asked *Floral Hat* once the Butler had receded beyond the trees.

"No doubt tossed into the trees in a fit of murderous pique by the crazed assailant," speculated *Van Dyke.*

"Should we search the woods for it?" asked *Clean-Shaven*, as I held my breath, willing them not to.

Floral Hat clutched her pearls, figuratively, "But what if the murderer is still gallivanting about out there, waiting for us?"

"Well, obviously the murderer is still about. We're all still here. Except for the butler, of course," Bernadette said.

"Didn't Sir Edward once talk of hiding things within the lining of his shoes?" *Souvarov* suddenly wondered aloud.

"Did he?" asked *Van Dyke*. "What an odd thing. Why would a man do that, I wonder? No, I don't believe that for a moment."

"Why, father! I believe you imparted that very anecdote about Sir Edward to Bernadette and me when we were but children," Virginia said, enthusiastically. "I remember you mentioning it while regaling us with stories of your travels together."

"*Did I?* Did I? Well!" harrumphed *Van Dyke*. "I suppose that might be possible."

I'm gonna take a brief pause in the action here, to briefly assay this ridiculous scene and to mention my recurring fear that I would one day somehow accidentally ingest one of Nouty Ned's concoctions, and subsequently find myself suffering hallucinations while wandering the forest. As I sat there, hiding under a tree in the snow, watching Masterpiece Theater jerk itself off in the woods, I became, like, 80 or 90 percent sure that this was exactly what had happened, although other theories I was considering included, but were not limited to: stumbling-upon-a-film-crew, time-travel, it's-all-a-dream, and fucking-rich-people-shit.

I decided that, hallucinations or no, these anachronisms had their murder well in hand, and that I could and should slip away in silence, rejoin Ned, then flee for home. Once there I could put on the police radio and find out if I needed to either come back or come down.

As quietly as I could, I made my way from the edge of the clearing, back through the woods. It was a bit of a maze and I was a bit light-headed, but I had a general sense of what direction we were in, and eventually found my way between the crowded trees. As I reached the clearing where I had left Ned, I could still hear voices on the breeze, though only as chittering noise, with nary an intelligible word, until the moment I realized that Ned was missing, his chair empty, followed immediately by a shout that rang out through the trees, clear as day, "GADZOOKS! AN ANARCHIST!"

"Fuuuuuuck," I moaned, before turning around, and hurrying back through the trees towards the scene of the crime.

I paused again at the edge of the clearing, hiding behind the final trees, peeking out between branches to see, sure enough, Nouty Ned standing in the clearing outside of the grove, pointing an accusatory finger at the party of people.

"—upper-class grande bourgeoisie bastards think you can keep the proletariat down, but your time will come and you'll be the first against the wall! Is this the day we rise up and fight back??? *IT MIGHT BE!*"

"No! Please not this day!" Virginia shrieked, as she cowered behind *Clean-Shaven*.

"See there! The rat admits to killing Sir Edward!" bellowed *Van Dyke*.

"Wait, he what now?" Ned replied, confused, bewildered, possibly tripping.

"Goodness! What a terrible fright this creature is!" exclaimed *Floral Hat*.

"Does he have a bomb?" Bernadette asked almost hopefully. "Most anarchists have bombs."

"We must apprehend him for the authorities!" shouted *Souvarov*.

"Get him, Michael! Prove your moxie and your love for my daughter by saving her from this creature!" *Van Dyke* gestured furiously with his fist towards Ned, no doubt wishing he had brought a brass cane or a bejewelled walking stick to shake as a cudgel.

"Um, get him?" Michael asked, "How? He's got a bomb."

"A bomb?!?" replied Ned, taken aback.

"He admits the bomb! The uprising is upon us! It begins here with the murder of Sir Edward, and it is encumbant upon us to end it here before this ruffian gets word back to his revolutionary brothers!" *Van Dyke* was on a roll. "For Queen and country, we must stop this man so that he may never murder again!"

"*What?!?* Hold on! Hold on!" Ned put his hands out as if to stop their accusations. "*Murder?*"

"The death of poor Sir Edward here is upon thy hands, anarchist!"

"Hey! I didn't murder anyone!" Ned stated back, "Wait — *is that a dead body?* Oh shit!"

"Father," Bernadette said cooly, putting her hand upon *Van Dyke's* arm. "I don't believe this man is our murderer most foul."

"Definitely not," Ned agreed.

"I'm not sure, Bernadette," *Souvarov* cautioned. "The coarse blood of the working class beast flows through his veins — men of his sort are capable of any sort of barbarous behaviour."

"Wow," Ned shook his head dolefully. "Really leaning into the whole 'patriarchy caste system thing', aren't we?"

Bernadette moved to stand between the enraged men and poor confused Ned. "And yet, are we not also capable of heinous crimes? Only we six, plus the butler, had avenue to this dagger lodged so tightly in the back and heart of poor Sir Edward."

At this, for some reason, Virginia let out a wail. "Ohhh, poor heart, it calls to me! Wicked! Divine! I can hide the truth no longer! Though I be betrothed to good Michael here, I have known the love of another!"

Gasp! Shock! Awe!

"Virginia! No!" Michael, eyes wide, covered his shame with his hands.

"Hush, girl. Not another word," commanded *Van Dyke*.

But Virginia could not be contained, "Yes! It's true! And what's more, I am carrying Sir Edward's baby! I had written to him of this information, but he had refused both my entreaty and all other missives, truly, he had ceased all communications as if he were some spectral phantom to me. I had thought him gone forever, until his appearance today, returned to our home in such haste, with such anger."

"Called it," Bernadette said, cooly.

"I am aghast!" declared Michael.

"Good lord, dear child! Whyever did you not confide in me? All problems have a solution if you know the right chemist!" *Floral Hat* took Virginia's hand and patted it comfortingly.

"I *demand* to know if you loved him!" Michael pressed.

"Here now! What is this all about?" a deep voice cut the party to silence, as a figure dressed in blue appeared on the path between the trees. "Your boy has summoned me to arrest a murderer and I find you…" he stopped, his mouth hanging open, as he saw Ned standing in the snow. "Uh… hello?"

"Hey," said Ned, only slightly more confused than the strangely dressed cop, "They murdered that dude over there."

I realized with a sharp shock that the constable was actually the butler wearing a strange buttoned blue uniform and a big fake mustache, and at that moment something clicked for me. I knew where I had seen him before, and I knew — or at least I really really hoped I knew — what was going on. I took a deep breath, crossed my fingers, and stepped from the trees, making my presence known. "*There* you are, Mortimer." I exclaimed to the falling mouths of the assembled party. I trudged through the snow to Ned. "Come now, we must away back to our meeting and leave these poor people alone. For now."

"And who, may I ask, are you?" *Van Dyke* asked in a huff.

"Pardon me, good sirs and ladies, I am the

good widow Ironheart, and I am chapter president of the local S.S.A.W. organization."

"S.S.A.W.?" asked Bernadette.

"The Society of Suffragists, Anarchists, and Wobblies, of course," I explained, curtly. "You should join us, dear. We have monthly meetups with assorted sweetmeats, stirring conversation, and, of course, plotting the downfall of the patriarchy. It is ever such a delight, and so much better for the complexion than bridge and needlepoint."

"Wow," whispered Bernadette.

"We were at a chapter meeting when Mortimer, who is a good man but a fiend for the mulled wine, fell into his cups and rushed off into the snow to start the revolution early." I smiled apologetically, as I took Ned by the arm. "Still, he is a pleasant enough chap when sober and even tight would not hurt a fly. I assure you that he could not have murdered your man there."

"Awww..." said the constable. "Thank you for seeing to your companion, and remember that temperance is a blessing bestowed on us by the lord."

"Looking out for our fellow man is the very cornerstone of our beliefs, officer." I nodded politely, then took a moment to spit at the body of Sir Edward, before holding out an outstretched fist and exclaiming, "SMASH THE PATRIARCHY AND EAT THE RICH!"

I then took Ned by the arm and firmly led him away from the scene as the players watched us go. Ned seemed too confused to act of his own accord, and I found myself bodily forcing him between the branches, the strange clearing with its birch trees and body, its stricken love stories and class warfare, quickly disappearing behind us as I hauled him back to where we had left our bags and chairs. By the time we got to our own little clearing, Nouty Ned had regained his footing, but not his voice.

We gathered the folding chairs and our bags in silence, but for the voices from the copse that still trickled past us on the breeze. were halfway back to the car before we couldn't hear anything else from the strange party and Ned finally broke the quiet. "Scrivener — what in the ever loving fuck was that?"

I burst out laughing, flooded by relief, and couldn't control myself enough to explain until we were getting warm back in the car.

"That..." I explained, "...was a murder party, Ned. At least that's my theory. The cop is actually a guy named, like, Curt? Chaz? No, not that — but something with a C — I'll look it up when I get home. Anyhow, I met him briefly last year when I reviewed a play he put on at the theater. I only met him the once, for the interview. So I guess he's working at, like, playacting mystery games? Anyhow, I'm *pretty* sure we stumbled into one of those."

"What? A mystery game?"

"Yeah, like, you get some friends, costumes optional, and then some actors present you with a mystery to solve. I'm guessing it's like that."

"Ohhhhh..." Ned nodded as it clicked, "They're, like, LARPing Clue[8]. Cool. Weird. I heard some screams, and you weren't there."

[8] Hey mom — LARP is an acronym for *Live Action Role Play*. You know those guys in the park dressed in cardboard armor whaling on each other with foam swords as they have the time of their lives? Those dudes are LARPing.

"I'd gone to investigate after I heard them, too, while you were asleep."

"Man," Ned chuckled, "Fucked me up when I wandered in on them."

"Yeah. It really threw me for a loop, as well."

"For awhile, I thought I might be tripping pretty hard out there…" Ned said, with an air of disappointment.

"Me, too, buddy. Me, too."

As we reached the outskirts of town, we stopped at a coffee and lunch place, and, realizing how cold I was, I got them to make me a hot cocoa brimming with whipped cream in a soup bowl. It was great.

While we were there, I poached their WiFi, searched around and, sure enough, found my man: Chris Cantrip, local theater and gaming professional. He had started a small side business — just until Kahnaway became the next national center of the theater, mind you — setting up and running live action mysteries for people, just like the one we had just encountered. There were a few off-the-shelf mysteries you could choose from, or you could order a customized one, with customer-provided details such as the era, characters, and location. You could even customize the victim, I guess for if you want to investigate the death of your ex or your boss or something. Interesting. I sent him a quick email explaining who had stumbled upon them that afternoon, while leaving out the bits about psychoactive experimentation, which seemed only prudent. Next, I dug up the area we had been in on various maps, and discovered that we had been a stone's throw from an old, abandoned manor — something too big to really call a house, which was unusual for our part of the world. Maybe it had recently been bought and renovated? I made a quick note about it. You never know what might be worth looking into at some point.

"Um, ma'am?" I looked up from my laptop as the waitress tapped me on the shoulder. "I think something is wrong with your friend over there."

I looked, and, sure enough, Nouty Ned was standing on a table, trying to grab imaginary butterflies or something from the sky, while humming through clenched teeth.

"Huh. I'll be damned, it worked," I said to no one, as I stood up and walked over to get him home before he hurt himself or got a real cop called on us.

Kahnaway, thus far:

Jiminy's BigFoot Tours — Jan, 2020

RIP, Granny Snickerdoodle — Feb, 2020

The Kaisershroom — Mar, 2020

Dealer Plates — Apr, 2020

Acornville — May, 2020

The Out Damned Spot Laundromat — Jun, 2020

D.B. Cooper's Underground Opium Emporium — Jul, 2020

Two Cabins — Aug, 2020

Redacted — Sep, 2020

Dick Procyon 4 Mayor —Oct, 2020

The Kahnaway Raccoonteurs —Nov, 2020

Top Ten Murdershrooms — Dec, 2020

A Trip Into Murder — Jan 2021

Kahnaway is a serialized novel being published monthly or thereabouts.

Make sure you get every episode by subscribing to Kahnaway at
patreon.com/calavara

Learn more about P. Calavara at Calavara.com and/or NeverKnows.com

Kahnaway — A Trip Into Murder
The Thirteenth episode of the Kahnaway series

by Polly & Perry Calavara

Kahnaway and Scrivener Jones © 2021
P. Calavara & Never Knows Books

Cover photo by Rick Perry
(the other Rick Perry, not the evil one)

Thirteenth episode, January 2021
First printing, January 2021

ISBN: 978-1-946296-34-4

Never Knows Books is a subsidiary of the Never Knows Heavy Manufacturing Concern